Unicorn Fri
Coloring & Acti

63 Unique designs
8 Activity Sheets

|Emerson Jade

Product of Emerson Jade

1
2
3
4
5
6
7
8
9
10
11
12
13
14
15
16
17
18
19
20
21
22
23

2
3
4
5
6
7
9
10
11
12
13
14
15
16
17

Help Sky Find Her
Missing Apple

3
2
4
1
5
6
7
8
9
10
13
11
12

Help Layla Find the Cupcake for Her Party!

Help Katie get to her friend Sadie

PYON = ___________

SRTA = ___________

RWNOIAB = ___________

OCRINNU = ___________

OSHER = ___________

IAGCIML = ___________

IERCEAMC = ___________

NUS = ___________

KDNI = ___________

AHLUG = ___________

LDUOSC = ___________

TOOC AYNCTDN = ___________

RSLGI = ___________

KAASCYTH = ___________

YNNSU = ___________

JYO = ___________

EPSEL = ___________

SOHUE = ___________

ECAK = ___________

EPI = ___________

KPSAELR = ___________

TESWE = ___________

PLEAP = ___________

PKACEUC = ___________

DIFERSN = ___________

ITLRGTE = ___________

AECCEIR M = ___________

BOONALL = ___________

PAHPY = ___________

ASELTC = ___________

BUBELBS = ___________

HTGIN = ___________

CDANY = ___________

ASRSG = ___________

SYK = ___________

ATRROC = ___________

SOOBK = ___________

OIOCKE = ___________

LLYLO = ___________

UFN = ___________

Solution

PYON	PONY	KPSAELR	SPARKLE
SRTA	STAR	TESWE	SWEET
RWNOIAB	RAINBOW	PLEAP	APPLE
OCRINNU	UNICORN	PKACEUC	CUPCAKE
OSHER	HORSE	DIFERSN	FRIENDS
IAGCIML	MIGICAL	ITLRGTE	GLITTER
IERCEAMC	ICE CREAM	AECCEIR M	ICE CREAM
NUS	SUN	BOONALL	BALLOON
KDNI	KIND	PAHPY	HAPPY
AHLUG	LAUGH	ASELTC	CASTLE
LDUOSC	CLOUDS	BUBELBS	BUBBLES
TOOC AYNCTDN	COTTON CANDY	HTGIN	NIGHT
RSLGI	GIRLS	CDANY	CANDY
KAASCYTH	HAYSTACK	ASRSG	GRASS
YNNSU	SUNNY	SYK	SKY
JYO	JOY	ATRROC	CARROT
EPSEL	SLEEP	SOOBK	BOOKS
SOHUE	HOUSE	OIOCKE	COOKIE
ECAK	CAKE	LLYLO	LOLLY
EPI	PIE	UFN	FUN

Made in the USA
Las Vegas, NV
21 March 2024

87522453R00072